For Seth and Aphra

B.M.

For Mara, Liz, Amelia and David

H.C.

First published 1987 by Walker Books Ltd, London
Text copyright © 1987 by Blake Morrison
Illustrations copyright © 1987 by Helen Craig

Library of Congress Cataloging-in-Publication Data
Morrison, Blake.
The yellow house.
Summary: A little girl's fascination with the
yellow house she passes each day leads her into
the garden which is full of fantastic surprises.
[1. Gardens—Fiction] I. Craig, Helen, ill. II. Title.
PZ7.M82927Ye 1987 [E] 87-7501
ISBN 0-15-299820-9

Printed and bound by L.E.G.O., Vicenza, Italy
First U.S. edition 1987   A B C D E

THE YELLOW HOUSE

WRITTEN BY BLAKE MORRISON

ILLUSTRATED BY HELEN CRAIG

HARCOURT BRACE JOVANOVICH, PUBLISHERS

SAN DIEGO   NEW YORK   LONDON

Every day we passed the yellow house
on our way to the park, Mom and
me and my little sister Jenny.
The house was on its own. It looked
old, sad and rather scary.

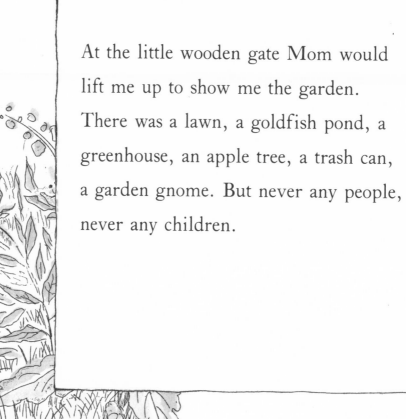

At the little wooden gate Mom would
lift me up to show me the garden.
There was a lawn, a goldfish pond, a
greenhouse, an apple tree, a trash can,
a garden gnome. But never any people,
never any children.

One day Jenny dropped her teddy near
the yellow house and Mom went back
to fetch it. I climbed the wooden gate
all by myself. Inside the garden was
a boy in overalls and a pom-pom hat.
He waved to me.

"Come inside!" he shouted.
"Come and play with me."

I pulled myself over and slid my legs down till they touched the pebbly path. The garden looked huge. The boy stood on the lawn.

"Come and see this!" he shouted.
"Come and see this."

I ran and looked. In the long grass
a tiger was playing with its cubs.
They cuffed and scratched each other.
They growled at me.

But the boy had moved off to the
goldfish pond.

"Come and see this!" he shouted.

"Come and see this."

I ran and looked. A white dolphin swam out from the lily pads, leapt in the air and splashed down on the water. It wiggled its tail at me.

But the boy had gone inside the greenhouse.

"Come and see this!" he shouted.

"Come and see this."

I ran and looked. A green snake was winding its body round the cane of a tomato plant. It shimmied and hissed. It stuck out its tongue at me.

But the boy was standing under the apple tree.

"Come and see this!" he shouted.

"Come and see this."

I ran and looked. A pelican was roosting
on a branch. It swallowed an apple with a
chomp chomp. It wobbled its pouch at me.

But the boy had opened the trash can.
"Come and see this!" he shouted.
"Come and see this."

I ran and looked. Inside the trash can
a panda was reading a newspaper.
It squinted and ho-hoed. It lifted its
hat when it saw me.

But the boy was striding through the
front door of the house.
"Come and see this!" he shouted.
"Come and see this."

I ran to look but the boy had closed the
door. I stretched and stretched, right up
on my tiptoes, but the handle was too
high for me. I rang the bell but no one
came to answer.

Now Mom had seen me and was calling
from the wooden gate. She looked cross.
I walked very slowly down the pebbly
path. Mom lifted me back over the gate.

"Where have you been?" she asked.
"Jenny was worried." Then Mom gave
me a great big kiss.

We still go past the yellow house on our way to the park, Mom and me and my little sister Jenny. Mom lifts me up to see the garden. There is a lawn, a goldfish pond, a greenhouse, an apple tree, a trash can, a garden gnome. Never any people though, never any children, never the boy who waved to me. But I know one day he'll be there again calling me in to play.